# Draw Dragon Dot Eyes

## and other Chinese Fables

Retold by Ellen Ching

Illustrations by
Xiao-Huan Li, Pi-chi Dodds,
and Jing Lili

**Starfall**®

This book is part of the
"I'm Reading!" fluent reading sequence
featured on

# www.starfall.com

See the *"Chinese Fables"* in the
*"I'm Reading"* section of the website.

ISBN: 978-1-59577-054-7

## Starfall Education
P.O. Box 359, Boulder, Colorado 80306

# Contents

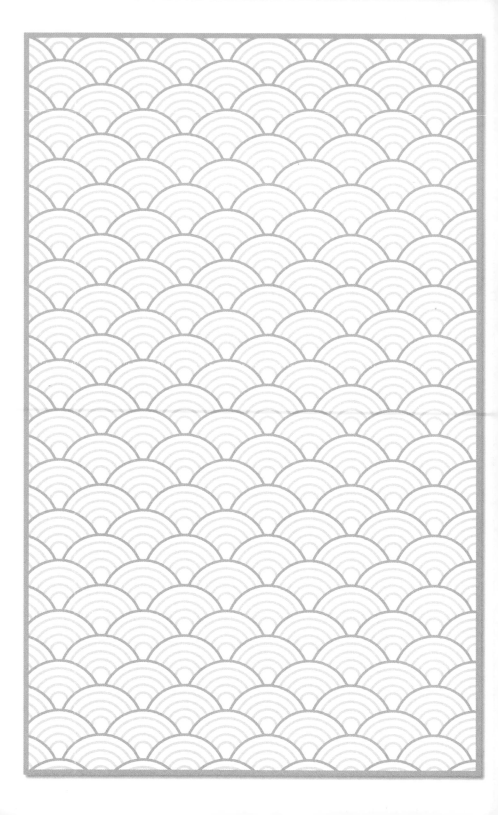

# Foreword
## For Parents and Teachers

This book contains six ancient Chinese fables. Among them, two stories—"One Rice Thousand Gold" and "Cup Bow Snake Reflection"— are based on alleged events. "Draw Dragon Dot Eyes" is a narrative written in an exaggerated way by an ancient writer. The other three — "Dung-Shi [1] Copies Eyebrows," "Yay-Gung Loves Dragons," and "Morning Three Night Four"—are creations of pure imagination.

All six fables originate from Chinese classics. "Dung-Shi Copies Eyebrows" and "Morning Three Night Four" come from *Zhuangzi* of the warring period (4th century B.C.E.). "One Rice Thousand Gold" can be traced to *The Records of Histories* written in the Han period. "Yay Gung Loves Dragons" is taken from the *New Preface*. "Cup Bow Snake Reflection" is from *Meanings of Customs*. The narrative of "Draw Dragon Dot Eyes" is borrowed directly from *Famous Paintings through the Ages* published in the Tang Period.

Choosing Chinese fables as the subject for a book intended to teach elementary English readers the process of reading is fresh and innovative. The ancient fables adapted for this collection are highly interesting, and are sure to stimulate readers' interest and motivation. The interpretations are faithful to the original works. Though simplified, the vivid illustrations and concise text elegantly communicate the philosophical idea of the ancient originals. In this way, young children will learn to read, and increase their awareness of the ancient Chinese culture at the same time. It is certain that this book will be greeted with applause.

*- Prof. Zhang Fan*
*Department of History,*
*Peking University*
*Beijing, China*
*October, 2006*

---

1 **Editor's Note:** The Chinese use Pin-Yin spelling to translate Chinese characters to the English alphabet. This does not correspond exactly to the conventional English phonetic spellings used in these stories. In the Pin-Yin system, *"Dung-Shi"* would be spelled *"Dong-Shi," "Shi-Shi"* would be *"Xi-Shi," "Sung-Yow"* would be *"Seng-Yao," "Yay-Gung"* would be *"Ye-Gong,"* and *"Han-Shin"* would be *"Han-Xin."*

# Introduction

"Draw Dragon Dot Eyes." A silly saying? Or an entire story in four words? The saying comes from an old Chinese fable with a very important lesson. The wisest men and women in China know many sayings like this one by heart. This includes two of the wisest women in the world: my grandmother, whom I sadly never had a chance to meet, and my mother.

When I was a little girl, I heard these fables from my mother. She heard them from *her* mother, who heard them from *her* mother and father. My mother didn't tell me all of the fables at once. Instead, she told one every time she wanted to teach me a very important lesson. At the dinner table. Before I fell asleep at night. When I didn't want to do my homework. When I was curled up in her arms.

These fables have been passed down from century to century—and now, from sea to sea. You will meet dragons and beautiful girls. You will meet monkeys and kind kings. As you will see, they are no different from you and me. That is why we can learn so much from them. And that is why children years from now will still learn from them. By writing down these fables in English[1], I hope to keep them alive. Not just the dragons and kings (though they will be happy to be remembered), but also the lessons they teach us all.

*(Continued...)*

---

[1] My mother told me these fables in her first language, Cantonese, a dialect from South China.

*(Introduction, continued...)*

In Chinese, just like in English, we use sayings to express ideas. English sayings such as "Do you have ants in your pants?" create funny pictures that help express a meaning. Of course, you don't *really* have ants in your pants! Sayings like these are called *idioms*. Chinese folk sayings go one step further. Full of history, fun to say, the sayings pack a whole story into four simple words![2]

Again, the wisest men and women in China know these sayings by heart. After reading these fables, you will be wise too!

*Ellen Ching*
*Cambridge, Massachusetts*
*April 6, 2005*

---

[2] Chinese idioms are often written in exactly four Chinese characters.

# Draw Dragon Dot Eyes

Sung-Yow had a secret.

He could paint a picture and make it come alive!

This happened only when the picture was finished.

Sung-Yow loved to paint
dragons. He left out their
eyes because he didn't want
them to come alive.

In this way, his secret stayed
a secret.

The king heard that Sung-Yow
was good at painting dragons.

He asked Sung-Yow to paint
four dragons on a wall.

In three days, the painting was *almost* finished.

The dragons looked like they could jump off the wall.

They didn't jump because Sung-Yow had left out their eyes.

People came from far away
to see the paintings.

"The dragons look so real!"
they said. "But where are
their eyes?" they asked.

"If I dotted the eyes, the dragons would fly away," said Sung-Yow.

Everyone laughed. No one believed him.

Sung-Yow was not happy.
This time he would *not* leave
out the eyes.

He painted little black dots
on two of the dragons.

Crash! Crack! The wall split
open. The two dragons
jumped off the wall.

Sung-Yow went on to
become a very famous artist
with a very famous secret.

*In China, when someone adds a finishing touch to their work, you might say:*

Draw

Dragon

Dot

Eyes

# Dung-Shi Copies Eyebrows

Shi-Shi was beautiful.

She was more beautiful
than the sun peeking over
the hills in the east.

Shi-Shi was more beautiful
than a pearl.

She was the most beautiful
girl in the world.

Shi-Shi was very kind and helped everyone.

When she saw a sad person, she put her hand over her heart and bent her eyebrows. Little wrinkles showed around her eyes.

When Shi-Shi walked by,
people bowed down and said,
"What a beautiful girl. She is
so kind."

Shi-Shi had a beautiful,
kind heart.

There was another girl, named Dung-Shi.

"I'm not very beautiful," said Dung-Shi as she looked into the mirror.

Dung-Shi wanted to be beautiful like Shi-Shi.

Dung-Shi had an idea.

"I will copy the way Shi-Shi looks. Then people will say that I am beautiful, too."

So Dung-Shi put her hand over her heart and bent her eyebrows.

When people saw Dung-Shi they said, "What a foolish girl. She is only pretending to be kind!"

No one said that Dung-Shi was beautiful.

What made Shi-Shi so beautiful? It was the kindness deep inside her heart that made her beautiful!

Dung-Shi copied Shi-Shi's eyebrows and wrinkles, but her heart was *not* really kind.

*In China, if you see someone poorly imitating another person, you might say:*

Dung-

Shi

Copies

Eyebrows

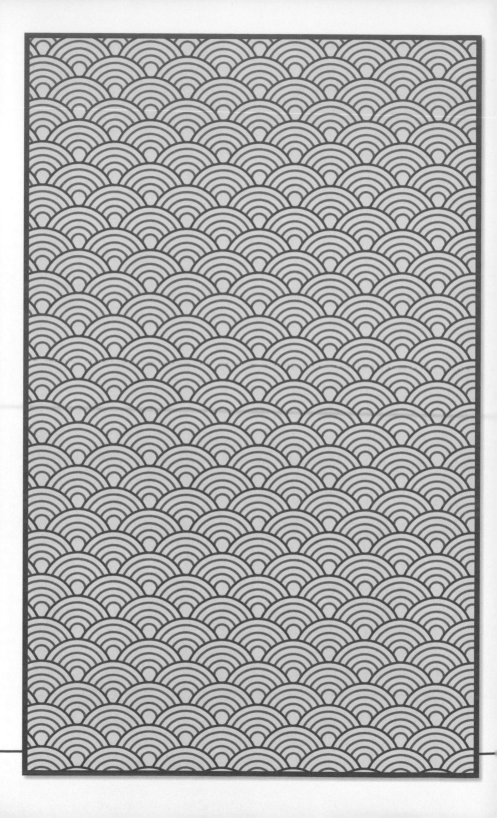

# Yay-Gung Loves Dragons

Yay-Gung loved dragons.

He loved to read about dragons.

He loved to think about dragons.

Yay-Gung loved dragons more than the desert loves rain.

He loved dragons more than a puppy loves to play.

Yay-Gung's house was full of dragons.

He even had dragons on his pajamas!

Yay-Gung wanted to see a *real* dragon.

He wished he could count the bumps on a dragon's tail.

A *real* dragon heard about Yay-Gung's wish.

The dragon hopped onto a cloud and floated down to meet Yay-Gung.

The dragon poked his nose into the bedroom window.

His tail curled around the house and hit the door!

"Who's there?" asked Yay-Gung.

He ran to the door and saw the dragon's tail!

He ran to the bedroom and
saw the dragon's nose.

Yay-Gung was afraid. He hid
under his bed. He shut his eyes
until the dragon went away!

Yay-Gung still loves dragons.
He loves to read about them.
He loves to think about
them. But...

Yay-Gung *never* wants to
see a *real* dragon again!

*In China, when you get something you thought you really wanted, but find out it wasn't as good as you expected, you might say:*

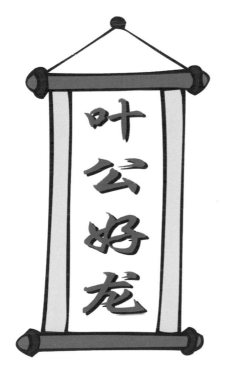

叶公好龙

Yay-

Gung

Loves

Dragons

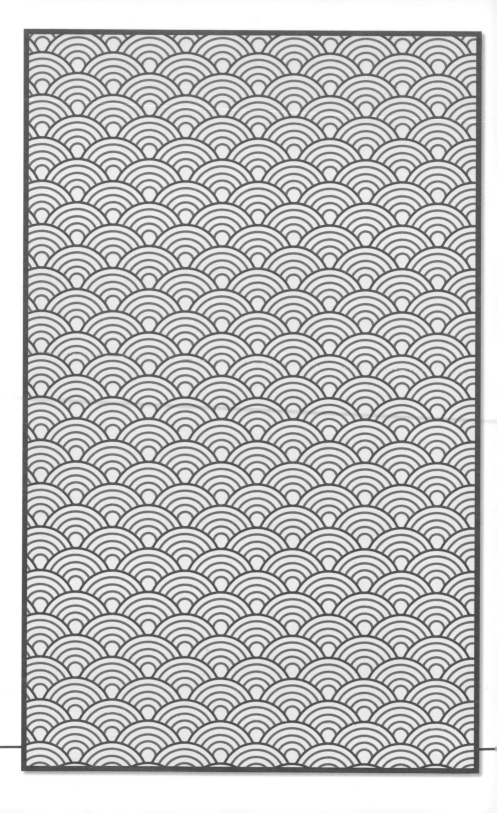

# One Rice Thousand Gold

Han-Shin was a very poor boy.

His family had nothing to eat.

Every day, Han-Shin went to the river to fish.

He sat and sat, but there were no fish.

One day, a few women were washing clothes in the river.

One old woman looked at Han-Shin.

"That boy is as skinny as the stick in his hand!" she said.

The old woman walked over to Han-Shin.

"You look hungry. Please eat this bowl of rice," she said.

Han-Shin bowed down.

"Thank you," he said.

Every day after that, the old woman gave Han-Shin a bowl of rice.

"I will find a way to pay you back," said Han-Shin.

When Han-Shin grew up, he became brave and kind.

He helped everyone.

The people loved him so much that they made him king!

Han-Shin and his family now had all the food they wanted.

But Han-Shin never forgot his promise to the old woman.

He looked far and wide to find her.

At last, Han-Shin found
the old woman.

He took her to his palace.

Han-Shin bowed down.

"I promised I would pay you back someday. Please take these thousand pieces of gold," he said.

He gave the old woman a bowl filled with *gold*!

"Thank you for the gold,"
said the old woman, "but
you've already paid me back
by becoming a strong and
kind man."

*In China, when someone repays another person's kindness with a rich reward, you might say:*

One

Rice

Thousand

Gold

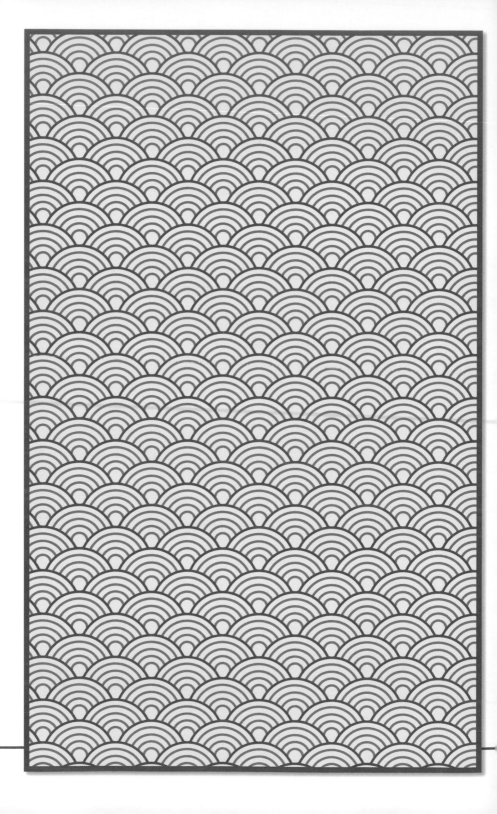

There once was a man who lived with monkeys.

He played with monkeys.

He even *talked* to monkcys!

The man loved the monkeys and treated them like his own children.

That's why he was called Papa Monkey.

Every day, Papa Monkey fed
bananas to his monkeys.

He fed them in the morning
and at night.

One day, Papa Monkey almost ran out of bananas.

He called his monkeys together.

"I'm sorry," he said, "but I can only give you *three* bananas in the *morning* and *four* bananas at *night*."

"Only *three* bananas in the
morning!" cried the monkeys.
"We want more!"

Papa Monkey had an idea.

"I will give you *four* bananas in the *morning* and *three* at *night*. How about that?" he said.

The monkeys yelled with joy,
"*Four* bananas in the morning!
That *is* much better!"

They kissed Papa Monkey.

What is *three* plus *four*?

What is *four* plus *three*?

The monkeys got the same
*seven* bananas a day!
They were just too silly
to see it.

*In China, when someone keeps changing their mind, you might say:*

Morning

Three

Night

Four

# Cup Bow
# Snake Reflection

Did you ever drink snake tea? Wang-Gung did!

One sunny day, Wang-Gung visited his friend.

He sat down and his friend gave him a cup of tea.

Wang-Gung looked in his cup.

Something was wiggling *inside*!

"There is a snake in my tea!"
he said to himself.

Wang-Gung's tummy did a little flip-flop.

He didn't want to hurt his friend's feelings, so he drank every drop of the tea!

The next day, Wang-Gung felt sick.

His tummy felt like it was doing cartwheels.

His face was as green as a tree.

Wang-Gung visited his friend again.

"There was a snake in my tea yesterday!" said Wang-Gung.

"That can't be!" said his friend.

Wang-Gung's friend took a
cup of tea and sat in the
same chair.

Something *was* wiggling inside
the cup of tea!

Quickly, his friend spun around in the chair.

"Now I see what made the snake appear!" he said.

*What* did he see?

There was a bow on the wall behind the chair. The bow's reflection wiggled in the tea, just like a snake!

Wang-Gung didn't feel sick anymore. But he did feel a little silly!

*In China, when a person is worrying about silly things that are not real, you might say:*

Cup

Bow

Snake

Reflection

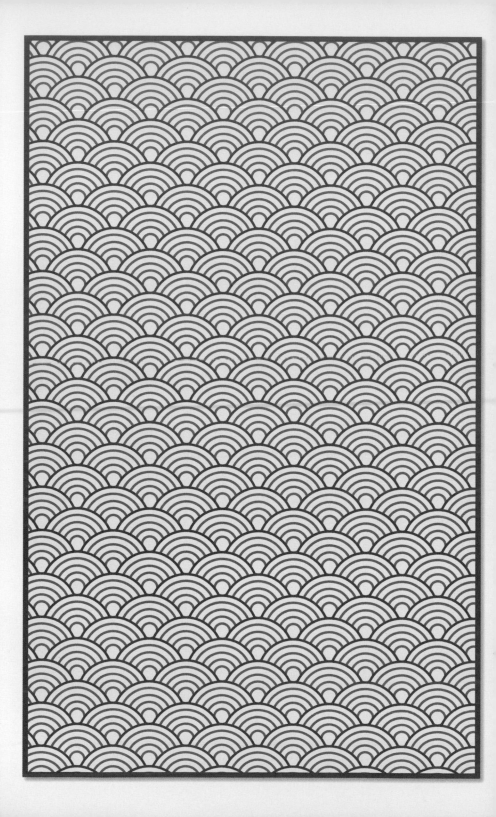